EVELYN DEL REY
IS MOVING AWAY

Meg Medina

illustrated by Sonia Sánchez

CANDLEWICK PRESS

As you read together, use the ideas below to help jumpstart your child's curiosity and foster essential early language skills.

Bring the Story to Life

- Make reading fun and interactive. Read expressively (use voices, gestures, and actions) to draw your child into the story and boost their understanding of events, characters, and themes.
- As you follow Daniela and Evelyn during their day together, explain new words, comment on illustrations, and ask questions.
- Mimic the actions of the characters, such as sneaking past the door, spinning in circles, or pressing a hand to your cheek.

Learn New Words

Providing a simple explanation for words that your child may not be familiar with can help build their language skills. You can describe the meaning of a word, point to an illustration, or use tone of voice to convey the word's meaning. Here are some words to talk about while you read *Evelyn Del Rey Is Moving Away*:

Bundle – to dress warmly

Gobble – to swallow or eat in a hurry

Sneak – to move quietly and secretly

Grouchy – when someone complains about things

Vanished – disappeared or gone away

Blur – something that you cannot see clearly

Promise – saying for certain you will do something or something will happen

Build Understanding

Asking questions and talking about the story as you read together can help your child make connections between the characters, their emotions, and the events in the story. As you read, try these tips to help boost your child's engagement and understanding:

- Before you begin the story, say, *"Today we will read a story about two best friends as they prepare for one of them to move away. I wonder how they will spend their day."*
- Talk about why this day in the story isn't just like any other day. Ask, *"What makes today different for Evelyn and Daniela?"*
- Make predictions in the story using "I" statements, like "I wonder" and "I think," to help build comprehension. You might say, *"I think Evelyn and Daniela's friendship is very special. I wonder how they will stay friends once Evelyn moves away. Let's keep reading to find out."*
- Ask questions and make comments that help your child identify and understand how characters are feeling. For example: *"Even though her mom reminds her that she will make new friends, Daniela feels sad that Evelyn won't be right there anymore. It's okay to feel sad when a friend moves away."* You can also point out Evelyn's face when she is in the car and ask, *"How do you think Evelyn is feeling now?"*
- Connect the story to something from your child's own experience. You might talk about someone you know who moved away and ask, *"What did we do to keep in touch?"*
- After you finish reading the story, turn to the end of the book to find additional questions and conversation starters.

To Kate Fletcher, who always helps me
find the way to the heart of a child's story
MM

For my friend Tania. Although I no longer see you each day,
I have you in my heart. You are my friend and my treasure.
SS

This is a work of fiction. Any similarities to real people, living or dead,
are coincidental and not used intentionally by the author or illustrator.

Text copyright © 2020 by Meg Medina
Illustrations copyright © 2020 by Sonia Sánchez

First edition 2020
This edition published specially for Jumpstart's *Read for the Record*® 2020 by Candlewick Press

Library of Congress Catalog Card Number pending
ISBN 978-1-5362-0704-0 (Candlewick trade English edition)
ISBN 978-1-5362-1334-8 (Candlewick trade Spanish edition)
ISBN 978-1-5362-1892-3 (Jumpstart Read for the Record® English edition)
ISBN 978-1-5362-1893-0 (Jumpstart Read for the Record® Spanish edition)

20 CCP 1

Printed in Shenzhen, Guangdong, China

This book was typeset in Avenir.
The illustrations were created digitally.

Candlewick Press
99 Dover Street
Somerville, Massachusetts 02144

www.candlewick.com

EVELYN DEL REY is my mejor
amiga, my número uno best friend.

"Come play, Daniela," she says,
just like she always does.

Just like today is any other day.

So I bundle up and cross the street.
A big truck with its mouth wide open is
parked at the curb, ready to gobble up
Evelyn's mirror with the stickers around
the edge, her easel for painting on rainy
days, and the sofa that we bounce on to
get to the moon.

She is waiting for me
inside the iron doors.

Then we climb the steps
two at a time,
just like we always do.

We sneak past grouchy Mr. Miller's door and wave to Mr. Soo, who's feeding pigeons from the hall window.

Señora Flores gives us each a cookie and says, "It's the big day!" when we walk by.

Our apartments are almost twins, just like us. That's why I already knew all the good places for hide-and-seek, and the spot behind the heater where we keep our special finds.

But the walls in Evelyn's room are sunny yellow, while mine are pink like cotton candy.

And I live with my mami and a hamster, and she has a mami, a papi, and a cat.

We are mostly the same,
just like our apartments.

But not after today.

We find a still-empty box near the door. In no time,
I am a bus driver steering us all over the city. We play
until the tables that were bus stops are gone and the
beds that were skyscrapers have vanished, too.

When we look around, everything has disappeared
except us.

Soon the truck outside
rumbles off, and there is
a knock on the door.

"Hide!" we say, giggling.
Just like we always do.

But our mothers see us
before we can slip away.
"Time to go," Mami says.

Evelyn and I hold hands in that wide empty space.
We lean back and start to spin in circles,
faster and faster, until everything is a blur around us.
Our fingers slip, but we don't let go until we wobble to the floor.

"We can talk every day after school," I tell her,
 though the world is still whirling.
"And you can visit me this summer," she says.
"And spend the night!"

But I know that tomorrow
everything will be different.

Evelyn will be in a new home
that doesn't match mine.

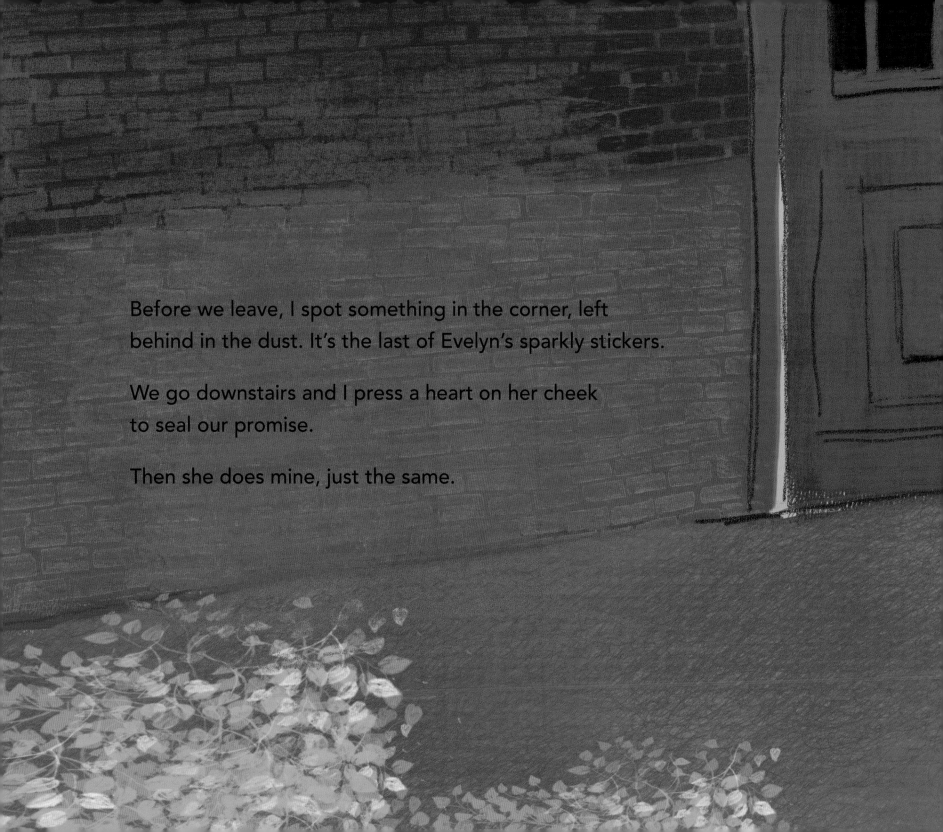

Before we leave, I spot something in the corner, left
behind in the dust. It's the last of Evelyn's sparkly stickers.

We go downstairs and I press a heart on her cheek
to seal our promise.

Then she does mine, just the same.

We say "¡Patata!" while Mami takes a photo.
We do our secret handshake one more time.

And then Evelyn hugs me hard.

Evelyn Del Rey is moving away.
So she won't be right here anymore.

Mami says not to be sad,
that we will both make new friends.

But when Evelyn waves one last time,
the stickers still on her cheeks,
I know she will always be my first mejor amiga,
my número uno best friend . . .

the one I will always know by heart.